The Big Sad

Author: **Lyndell Clark**
Co-Author: **Taylor Ross**

To order additional copies of this book, contact:
Xlibris
AU TFN: 1 800 844 927 (Toll Free inside Australia)
AU Local: 0283 108 187 (+61 2 8310 8187 from outside Australia)
www.xlibris.com.au
Orders@Xlibris.com.au

ISBN: Softcover   978-1-6641-0173-9
          EBook   978-1-6641-0174-6

Print information available on the last page

Rev. date: 11/12/2020

The Big Sad

Bentley Bunny was a lot like other bunnies his age.

He had a mum and dad who loved him, and he loved them. His dad worked hard and was a very busy bunny. Bentley liked to talk a lot, so his dad was sometimes too tired to listen to all of Bentley's ideas at the end of the day.

His mum worked hard too, but Bentley knew his mum would always listen to what he had to say and try to understand him. What Bentley didn't know was that they were very much alike.

Bentley was the baby of his family. Sometimes he felt like his family didn't really notice him or listen to what he said. He felt a little bit different to everyone else.

He had two brothers. His oldest brother, Boris, was very confident and always seemed to have the answer to any question Bentley asked. Bentley wished he could be as confident as his big brother, but he wasn't.

His next oldest brother, Buster, was strong and muscly and wasn't scared of anything! Buster was a torment, and at times Bentley wished that, just once, he could be tougher than Buster!

Bentley had a lot of good friends and always tried very hard to listen to their problems and help out when he could. Bentley always tried to see the positive in any situation and felt responsible for keeping everyone happy.

He was a very funny bunny and made the other bunnies laugh a lot.

Bentley had clever ideas and liked learning new things.

What other bunnies didn't realise was that Bentley had a secret. He seemed like other bunnies, but inside of him there was a worried little dark spot that he called "the Big Sad."

When Bentley first noticed the Big Sad, it wasn't really that big at all. It was a little dreary voice that pointed out things that were scary, or bad, or that could go wrong. At first Bentley told the voice that it was wrong. The Sad would go away for a while and keep quiet.

But just when Bentley thought it was gone, the Sad would come back.

The Sad would follow him to school and point out the mistakes that he made—even the little ones. The Sad would make Bentley feel that he was weird or different and that he wasn't good enough for those around him. Every time the Sad spoke, its voice grew bigger and bigger.

The Sad would even talk over Bentley's friends when they spoke, and before long it was the only voice that Bentley noticed.

Bentley especially loved to draw; it was something he was very proud of! But the Sad told him that his friends' drawings were better than his own.

Bentley sometimes hid alone to escape from what the Big Sad told him, and other days the Big Sad made Bentley feel mad, but mostly, it made Bentley feel as if he was all alone.

The Sad grew and grew as Bentley heard it talking more and more about things that could or had gone wrong throughout his day. Even when Bentley told it to be quiet, the Sad never stopped talking!

The Big Sad always believed it was right and was only afraid of a few things.

The Big Sad did not like being questioned, it did not like being told "no", and most of all, it did not like Bentley telling others what it had said.

One day Bentley couldn't take the Big Sad any longer, so he went and told his mum what it had told him. Bentley was so worried this would somehow make the Big Sad madder, but to his surprise, his mum said she had also met the Big Sad and knew what it felt like to have it come and stay.

She said that the Big Sad hated it when we told it to be quiet and assured Bentley that it didn't ever tell the truth. So, Bentley tried telling the Big Sad that it was a liar. He told it to be quiet, and the Big Sad got a bit smaller.

The Big Sad had lots of tricks. It loved to make it seem like Bentley's thoughts and choices could make everyone's problems bigger. This made Bentley scared to even come out of his room. But Bentley's mum knew that the Big Sad wasn't telling the truth.

The Big Sad didn't like Bentley's mum and kept trying hard to be heard. She had already won battles with the Big Sad and knew what to do!

Bentley's mum would often ask Bentley, "What's the worst thing that could happen?" He would stop and think, then realise that some of the Big Sad's ideas were pretty crazy. Mum knew the things the Big Sad said were made smaller by telling others about it, so she asked Bentley's brothers to help him win his battle with the Big Sad.

Boris and Bentley were very close, and Bentley felt he could tell Boris anything. Boris listened and told Bentley that he could fight the Big Sad by using his strengths. He could shrink the Big Sad by telling it the truth. Bentley tried this and told the Big Sad about his great report from school—and it shrunk a little! Boris told Bentley that he should talk to Buster. Buster was a strong bunny, but he hadn't always been strong.

Bentley went to Buster and told him about the Big Sad. Buster, who was usually tough and cranky, hugged Bentley because he had been bullied by the Big Sad for years. He told Bentley that the toughest part of his body wasn't his muscles, but his mind—and the Big Sad is *not* the boss of your mind! Bentley had found his confidence and his strength and was ready to face the Big Sad because he had finally realised that he wasn't alone.

Bentley went to his dad and told him about the Big Sad. Bentley's dad told him that his entire family was on his side. He also told Bentley about a special doctor who could help him win the fight against the Big Sad.

They made an appointment with the special doctor who knew about the Big Sad. Realising that he was not the only one to face the Big Sad filled Bentley's heart with hope.

Having someone listen to and understand him made Bentley feel better. He felt free to talk because no one he talked to ever felt mad or sad about what he said. Bentley was able to say everything he felt—even if he knew it was silly!

At school, Bentley noticed he wasn't the only worried bunny! He saw other worried bunnies everywhere, some alone, some hiding, and some creating crazy bunny mischief. Bentley started to realise he was not the only bunny that the Big Sad annoyed. The Big Sad annoyed heaps of bunnies! Bentley realised that others were feeling like he had and that some people had even beaten the Big Sad!

Bentley had seen that the Big Sad wanted everyone to feel out of control, but Bentley's family had taught him that he could control his brain and choose what it believed! He learnt if we think bad things, it hurts our brains. But if we tell our brains good things, it grows stronger!

So, Bentley began to stand up to the Big Sad by saying, "I am a normal bunny"—and "mistakes are how we learn." As Bentley's voice grew stronger and more confident, the Big Sad's voice grew weaker and quieter. Bentley wasn't always free of the Big Sad's company, but as he continued to fight it with the truth the Big Sad became less noticeable.

As time passed and Bentley kept fighting back, the Big Sad got quieter, less frequent, and less scary! Sometimes, Bentley would hear the Big Sad's whispers, but he realised that the Big Sad was not his friend—it had hurt him, and it didn't want him to be happy! Bentley's family had joined together to show the Big Sad that it was not welcome in their lives ever again!

Bentley was a talented bunny. He had a family who loved him and whom he loved. He was great at drawing, and though he wasn't perfect, he was a normal bunny. Bentley was the boss of his brain, and he had a bright future ahead of him. Bentley realised he would need others to support and understand him, but that is what family is for. His brothers had their own talents, but Bentley was unique and talented in a very different way. Bentley was perfect just the way he was!

CPSIA information can be obtained
at www.ICGtesting.com
Printed in the USA
BVHW020255301220
596687BV00001B/13